The Wondrous Journeys
of
Peter and Wapahoo

by Traci K. O'Reilly

RoseDog 🐾 Books

PITTSBURGH, PENNSYLVANIA 15222

ISBN: 978-1-4349-9797-5
Printed in the United States of America

First Printing

For more information or to order additional books,
please contact:
RoseDog Books
701 Smithfield Street
Pittsburgh, Pennsylvania 15222
U.S.A.
1-800-834-1803
www.rosedogbookstore.com

Dedication

I want to thank my husband, Sean O'Reilly, for all the help and support during the writing of this book. I also want to thank our three sons, Randy, Colton, and Spencer O'Reilly. They were the inspiration in writing this book.

I'd also like to thank my mother, Dorothy Lennon, for listening to all of my rough drafts and for the support. And finally, I'd like to acknowledge my dear grandmother, Dollie M. Allen, who had such talent as a writer but was never able to have her writing published.

Contents

Chapter One

Wapahoo's Quest for Manhood

The year was 1832, a grand year to become a man. Wapahoo was a full-blooded Yurok Indian from the north, and he was about fifteen years of age. He was large in stature and about as handsome a devil as the Good Lord could make any young buck. Why, it has been said that all the young Indian maidens blushed with excitement when they saw Wapahoo, hoping he would be kind and interested enough to smile at them and offer to carry their water jugs back from the Klamath River. But the girls would have to wait for any romance they might be dreaming of, as Wapahoo was consumed with how the events of the next day would unfold.

Wapahoo was excited, but his stomach was upset, making gurgling, rumbling noises. He aimed his rump to the fire and let out a big blast of gas—whoosh! The flames of the fire blew higher. Wapahoo's baby sister yelled out as if the camp was under attack from the Tolowa. Wapahoo laughed hysterically and buried his head in his bear skin blanket to muffle the sound of his laughter.

"Shush," said Mother Shi-kies and said something not so nice in native tongue. "Oh, I wish the young girls could see you now. They might not think you are such a prize for a young buck."

Wapahoo composed himself. Sitting up and looking across the fire at Shi-kies, he asked, "Do you think I will spear an elk tomorrow?" as he pulled his deerskin pants and worn-out moccasins off. Shi-kies was busying herself with putting Wapahoo's baby sister to bed.

"I don't know, the elk are mean spirits. They don't want to be at the end of your spear. I will ask the great spirit to watch and protect you." Mother sighed. "Now go to sleep. Morning comes early."

Morning did come early—too early. Wapahoo had but a few minutes to dress. The warriors were anxious to be on the trail to the elk. There was a heavy dew on the ground and when Wapahoo's feet hit it, down he went, soaking his whole backside. Mother let out a big belly laugh while Wapahoo picked himself up and mounted his horse, his face bright red from embarrassment. The warriors laughed and uttered among themselves, "This is the young buck who will someday lead our tribe?"

A young girl about twelve years old was too smitten to be put off by Wapahoo's mishap. She smiled and waved goodbye as the warriors rode single file through the redwoods to the trail of the elk.

The horses prodded along the trail unenthusiastically. Wapahoo turned to a brave called Hurt Weasel and begin a conversation. He didn't get but two sentences out when Hurt Weasel halted his horse, looked Wapahoo straight in the eye, and said, "It is best to be quiet, so the great spirit can think of what he will do with you today."

Wapahoo looked at the ground, humiliated, and said to himself, "Today is not starting well."

Soon the small band was overlooking the majestic herd about twenty yards from where they stood. It was a sight to behold, and Wapahoo was quick to point out the elk he planned to shoot. If he brought down the huge elk, he would earn his manhood. If he didn't, well, then he would be shamed. He would then be sent on his second quest, but only if he succeeded on the second quest would he be shamed no more.

Without waiting for the signal, Wapahoo bolted forward toward the herd, leaving the warriors with dust in their eyes—well, that was his first mistake. His second was that he ran his horse right down into the middle of the herd. The herd began to panic. In all the frenzy, one bull elk fell to the ground, knocking Wapahoo and his horse to the ground. He didn't stop to think of the danger he was in. He grabbed the antlers of the massive elk and swung himself up on his back, and I swear this to be true, he rode that fella for a good fifteen yards. He got thrown, of course, after the stupid beast figured he had a passenger, but Wapahoo was still intact after he hit the ground and a smile as big as a river on his dirty face.

Signed, Peter Thornton
Age twelve years old
June 2, 1832

3

Chapter Two

Bobcat Hunt

Well, it wasn't easy to ride a full-grown elk, but Wapahoo figured he was up for the next challenge of becoming a man. He had his instructions from Chief Ha-go-i-neigh to go on a hunt for the bobcat, stay through the night with the bobcat's spirit, travel through Tolowa territory, and then return home. So Wapahoo gathered the necessities he would need for the hunt and left just before the sun came up.

He traveled on for many miles, and he was in high country now. He came to a crystal-clear river, plunged his spear into the sparkling blue water at the trout just below the surface, and missed the trout by a long shot. Wapahoo concentrated. He closed his eyes, imagining himself eating the trout. He was focused. He raised his spear and again plunged it into the icy river, pulling out a good six-inch trout. He let out a mighty chant of victory, bit the head off, and ate the fish raw.

Along the way of his journey, he saw all the animal life you could imagine but nothing that came next to a bobcat. He moved higher up in the woods and was now in the thickest part. Just about twenty-five feet from where Wapahoo was standing was an adult bobcat feeding on his kill of rabbit. He lowered himself to the ground and crawled closer, enough to get a clear shot. The bobcat caught the scent of him and stood growling, exposing his two-and-a-half-inch teeth, hissing wickedly. Wapahoo drew his bow and arrow. The cat whirled around and he shot him in the hindquarters. He darted away from Wapahoo and his kill. He charged after the fierce cat. The cat stopped in his tracks and turned to take Wapahoo on in his last attempt to survive. Wapahoo had but a moment to think. He reached for his arrows, but they weren't in his sack! They must have fallen out while he was running. The cat let out a ferocious scream to be heard throughout the forest. The birds in the tree took flight, making the situation all the more frightening.

The bobcat was once again the predator. He began closing in on Wapahoo. Wapahoo backed up and scoured the ground for his arrows. A yard from where he stood was one arrow. He retrieved it with amazing speed. He then lay down on the ground and positioned the bow and arrow on his chest to give him a direct shot when the cat attacked. The cat leapt into the air at Wapahoo. He launched the arrow mid-center, piercing the bobcat in the heart, blood spilling onto Wapahoo's face. The cat swiped Wapahoo's neck with his paw, let out one last fatal scream, and fell dead on top of Wapahoo.

Well, Wapahoo hadn't figured he would get injured. He had to find a stream with mud to pack the open wound. He realized he was in danger of losing too much blood. Luckily for Wapahoo, a stream was not far off, and he quickly searched the area for any of the necessary components to cover the wound. He then mixed it with mud. Wapahoo began to stagger and fell to the ground, unconscious.

Hours had passed, and a pair of juvenile otters were curious of the human lying on the shore. They brazenly approached and began nibbling at his feet. Wapahoo shifted his weight and kicked off the intruders unconsciously. The otters scrambled back to the water but soon were up on the shore again, ransacking Wapahoo's pockets and chewing on his leather pants. They could smell the fish he had caught earlier and were sure there was a fish underneath Wapahoo's leather pants. The games were over for the otters. They wanted free food. One bit down on Wapahoo's leg, and Wapahoo came to in excruciating pain. He yelled out, jumped to his feet, and kicked at the otters with all the strength he could muster. He didn't get a direct hit because the otters were back in the water, down stream and long gone. It took a few moments to figure what had happened, but then Wapahoo had to chuckle to himself. He had a special spot in his heart for otters and their antics. Luckily the bite from the otter was only a surface wound—nothing to worry about, Wapahoo figured—but he packed the bite on his leg with some mud just in case.

All was good for now. The sun was beginning to fade. Wapahoo gathered firewood and began skinning the mighty cat, cutting out the heart and liver to eat first, and it did tasted mighty good to a boy who had succeeded this time. The far-off howling of coyotes was a bit eerie, Wapahoo thought, but he would never let anyone know how scared he was becoming. The woods began to grow with howls, growling, and the sound of a hoot owl that stood perched in a nearby tree. The owl seemed interested in Wapahoo's meal of bobcat, but for now the owl seemed content at watching him and any other movement on the ground.

Wapahoo gathered his firewood and started a fire. He figured it would be a long night of uncertainty as to what animals might be lurking in the dark. He lay down and observed the stars shooting across the sky, and he was in awe of how clear the sky was on this night. He closed his eyes and drifted to sleep. It wasn't long before there was wrestling of the leaves and bushes just a few feet from his fire. Whatever it was, it must have smelled the bobcat meat. A pair of glowing eyes peered from behind the bushes. A lone older wolf leapt into the air and landed on top of Wapahoo, tearing away part of his shoulder's flesh. He cried out in agony, pulled the knife from his pouch, and stabbed the wolf repeatedly, until the wolf breathed no more.

Bloody and wounded, Wapahoo did what he could to patch himself up. He had a porcupine quill used as a needle, and he began to sew up the deep slash made by the wolf. He did what he could to bandage the wound with an extra rawhide shirt he had brought. He skinned the wolf and offered the wise owl some meat, for he thought the owl must have brought him good luck to be able to slay the wolf so effortlessly.

Wapahoo yawned. He thought to himself that he would have many scars to prove him a man and to show of his experiences in his quest for manhood. But for now, he hurt like a chicken with his head cut off!

He yawned and quite frankly was exhausted. He just didn't have another fight left in him. Wapahoo curled up by the fire once again. The moonlight and stars were still brightly displayed across the sky. The dried leaves crunched as someone or something approached. He figured he'd best be prepared this time. His spear in hand, he was ready for what awaited him. A black bear barreled out from behind a tree and stood up on his hind legs, snorting and growling, slapping the air with his magnificent paw. Wapahoo did the wisest and smartest move; he threw the wolf carcass at the bear and sped to the nearest tree. The bear sniffed the wolf and wandered off. It was too dangerous to sleep on the ground, he figured, so he slept in the tree the rest of the night.

Chapter Three
Traveling through Enemy Territory

Wapahoo climbed a ridge that looked over the valley. He was nervous and sweating, as he was in Tolowa territory. The Tolowa and Yurok had been at war for many years. Both tribes were known for stealing women and children. Many gruesome stories were told about how barbaric the Tolowa were to the women and children they captured. He knew he had to get to Yurok territory without being seen. The wolf and bobcat skins were heavy and itchy. Wapahoo would roll the skins up and hold them on top of his head for a while. He imagined being able to go on the next hunting party to kill the Tolowa.

Wapahoo let his guard down, his instincts dulled from exhaustion. He stumbled. He was being watched. He picked himself up and quickened his pace. He could hear the crunching of leaves from under someone's feet. He could hear the rattle of a rattlesnake, but he did not see it. At that moment, at an arrow flew down and punctured the snake in the head.

Wapahoo turned to his right to see a brave not much older than himself holding a knife. Wapahoo jolted forward in an attempt to get away. The brave threw his knife, striking Wapahoo in the calf. He fell to the ground. He was sure he would never see his people again.

The brave approached and grunted. He pulled Wapahoo up by the hair of the head and pulled the knife from his bleeding leg. He put the knife to Wapahoo's throat and clutched his hair, dragging him toward the Tolowa camp. Wapahoo had lost enough blood that he passed out. The brave grunted and tossed him over his shoulder with ease.

Wapahoo awoke in a wood plank house, his leg bandaged. A young maiden sat staring at him from across the room. She arose and handed him some water and some dried elk meat. Wapahoo hadn't eaten for some time, and he gladly accepted the food. He watched the girl move gracefully across the room and recognized her to be Nay Snusie. She was stolen from the Yurok three years ago. The tribe never knew what happened to her.

She had grown into an attractive girl, a little older than Wapahoo. She was slim and buxom. He smiled at her, speaking her name. He was overcome with emotion. He threw his arms around her and kissed her cheek.

Nay Snusie became indignant. She bit him on the lip and pushed him to the ground. Wapahoo wiped the blood dripping down his chin and spoke her name softly. Nay Snusie did not respond; she got up off her knees and left the shank house.

It was a burst of enthusiasm for Wapahoo. He was in love. He figured the Tolowa might let him live until the next afternoon, if that long. He waited until the village was quiet, and he quickly snuck out to his freedom. He could not figure why he was able to escape. Perhaps Nay Snusie let him leave.

Wapahoo walked home to the light of the moon. He had lost his bobcat and wolf skin, but that meant little to him after he about lost his life. The sun was up now, and Wapahoo looked out from behind the trees at his tribe ahead, feeling he had grown many years in these last two days.

He arrived home. The only one awake this early was Grandfather, sitting by the fire.

"Wapahoo!" Grandfather exclaimed. "We didn't know if we were going to see our young buck again. You have been gone for three days. Chief Ha-go-I-neigh was planning a search party to look for you today!"

Wapahoo told Grandfather of the incidences of the last three days and that the Tolowa had Nay Snusie.

"Did she look well?" asked Grandfather.

"She does not remember me, Grandfather. She had a scar on her left cheek about five inches long," said Wapahoo.

"She probably tried to run from the Tolowa and they branded her so no one would want her," Grandfather said, messing up Wapahoo's hair and stating proudly, "I've never known anyone to escape the Tolowa. You have become a great warrior when so many dangers awaited you."

Wapahoo became distraught.

"What is it, grandson?" Grandfather asked.

Wapahoo answered, "I will take Nay Snusie from the Tolowa. I will bring her home." It was a gut feeling he had, though he did not know when.

Chapter Four

Baptist Followers on Yurok Land

Wapahoo was awakened by the tribe members. There was fear. Wapahoo asked an elder what was the matter.

"There are wagons in the clearing and about thirty white people, men, women, and children," said the elder.

Wapahoo looked to the clearing and observed the wagons were pulled by steer, massive beasts with horns. Animals Wapahoo had never seen before. He was baffled by the strangeness of the animal. Wapahoo and five other warriors were chosen to accompany Chief Ha-go-I-neigh to speak to the white settlers.

A stout light-haired man stepped forward toward Chief Ha-go-I-neigh. He extended his hand and introduced himself as a Baptist minister. "Hello. My name is Sam Tyler. We would like to ask your permission to water our stock and kill some game before we travel on."

The chief had never had much association with the whites, and he felt they were not a threat to his people. "You may stay up to a week. Wapahoo will help you water your animals, kill game, and show you where the river is," stated the chief in a matter-of-fact tone.

The minister patted Wapahoo on the shoulder and introduced him to a blond boy. "This is Peter. He is a bit rambunctious. He will help you, Wi-pu-hu—is that the way you pronounce your name, son?" asked the minister.

Wapahoo didn't quite understand his words, but he knew "Wi-pu-hu" wasn't said correctly, so he said his name again.

"Wapahoo, got it," stated Sam Tyler.

Peter smiled weakly at Wapahoo. He found he was somewhat afraid of Wapahoo, maybe because of his brown skin and black eyes. "A real live Indian," Peter says to himself.

Yet Wapahoo didn't think much of the skin tone of Peter, but he sure thought Peter's crystal-blue eyes were about as blue as the sky. The corners of Wapahoo's mouth turned up until it was apparent he was smiling at Peter. Peter burst into the most exuberant toothy grin, as he had lost one of his front teeth when a horse ran away with him when he was eight years old. Both of the boys had twinkles in their eyes. Could they have sensed this was about to become one of the most significant friendships of their lives?

Peter mounted the old nag they called "Bolts" with a small wagon attached. The empty jugs were lying in back for the water they were to bring back. They rode a spell, each too nervous to ask the first question.

Peter could hear the rush of water not far off. Finally Peter asked a daring question, "Have you ever scalped another Indian?"

Wapahoo was relieved that words were finally being spoken. He was tired of the silence. Wapahoo replied, "No, but soon I will ride with the war party to kill the Tolowa."

Peter imagined being able to ride in the war party with real Indians. "You sure are lucky. I would love to go on a war party," said Peter.

Soon they were at the river. The boys dismounted. Wapahoo began to relax a little, and both boys quickly forgot the task at hand. Peter got a look of mischief in his eyes and splashed water on Wapahoo's face. Peter searched Wapahoo's expression. He didn't know what Wapahoo was going to do. Wapahoo smiled and pushed Peter into the water. Peter jutted out of the water and tackled him. They fell into the water laughing. They wrestled in the water while trying to stay afloat, all the while testing each other's strength. Soon the boys tired of the game.

"We need to find something for you to eat tonight," Wapahoo said to Peter.

Peter smiled his wide toothy grin as he mounted his horse. He felt like he was reading a book, and he and Wapahoo were the main characters, handsome and dashing. The thrill of the moments he had already encountered were surreal. "Someday," Peter said to himself, "I will write a book about my adventures!" Little did he know what a role Wapahoo would play in his book.

They rode a spell, and Wapahoo whispered to Peter, "Maybe we will find an elk or a deer soon."

They dismounted their horses and tied them up the nearest tree. They set out on foot. It was midday and already over one hundred degrees. The boys sat in the shade saying nothing, observing any movement. Then a doe stepped out from behind the trees about fifteen yards away. Wapahoo told Peter to sit and wait. Wapahoo scrunched down and headed for a young oak tree not far from the deer. The doe was oblivious of him and continued to graze, flicking her tail back and forth nervously. Wapahoo drew his bow and arrow and released, striking the doe in the neck. Wapahoo chanted, raising his bow and arrow in the air and letting out a yell. He motioned Peter to him, and then he began to gut the deer. A fawn stepped out, looking to be a couple of days old. Well, neither boy reckoned with taking a fawn home. Both boys, being kindhearted souls, carefully approached the fawn and scooped him up in their arms to take back to camp.

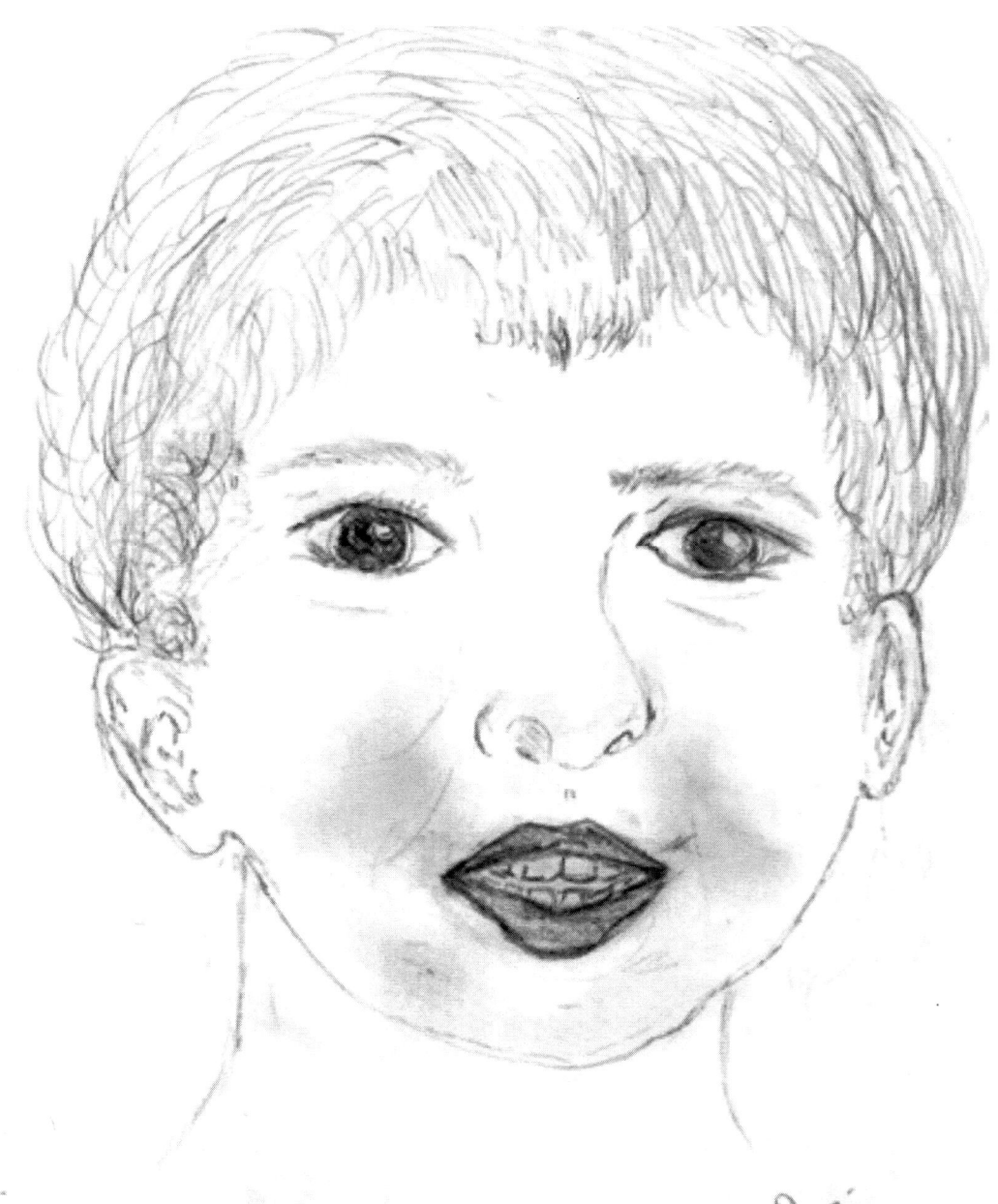

"Hey, Wapahoo, bet you didn't think we would get two deer today, did ya?"

"Wow, who'd a thunk it!" said Peter. He carried the fawn to the wagon as Wapahoo finished gutting the deer and put it in the back of the wagon.

Peter lifted the tiny fawn up to Wapahoo.

"I'll ride ahead," said Wapahoo.

The boys took every measure so that the fawn would not see his dead mother. The elders skinned the deer and hung it by the buttocks to make the meat tender and flavorful. Peter was given his share of the meat and then rode back to his camp. Wapahoo pet the little deer and began to pick the ticks out of his fur. He had yet to come up with an idea on how to feed the fawn.

Chapter Five

Look Yonder, 'Tis a Goat!

Wapahoo looked across the field to the wagon train. There was Peter, pulling a very unwilling goat.

"I thought you could use this cranky old varmint!" cried Peter excitedly.

Wapahoo cried out ecstatically, "I didn't know how we were going to feed the little fawn!"

Peter was proud he could be of assistance. All the while, the fawn struggled to catch up to Wapahoo.

"Just one thing I got to tell ya. Be careful when you bend over. She kind of likes to butt folks. She's known in Kansas for a lot of black-and-blue rumps, skinned-up noses and knees."

They led the fawn to the goat's teats. It was nothing doing for the goat. She turned and butted the fawn a couple of feet.

"Well, she ain't gonna let the fawn anywhere near her." Peter stepped back and scratched his head, thinking for a moment. "Well, the next best thing is a baby bottle!" said Peter.

Wapahoo looked puzzled. "What's a baby bottle?"

Peter sprinted toward the wagon. He yelled over his shoulder, "I'll show you in a minute!"

Wapahoo watched Peter disappear into a wagon, and out he jumped, holding something in his hand. Peter ran the whole way back to Wapahoo, sweating and out of breath.

"This, my friend, is a baby bottle!" Peter said proudly. "The goat is used to getting milked. That's about all she is good for, 'cause it ain't her disposition," sighed Peter. "Oh, now don't forget, don't bend over or she'll butt you into the next county."

The boys milked the goat and poured it into the bottle. Peter, being raised on a farm, took over.

"This is how you do it. You put just a taste on their lips to see if they like it."

The fawn licked his muzzle, and it was obvious he was very hungry. Peter pressed the nipple into the fawn's mouth, and he suckled the nipple and drank eagerly until the milk was gone.

Peter explained, "You can't feed him more than one bottle at a time or it will make him sick."

The fawn folded his little legs beneath him and lay down to sleep.

"How about we call him Ned?" asked Peter.

"Okay," said Wapahoo.

"The goat, her name is Sally," said Peter. Peter got to thinking. "Hey, why don't I stay overnight with tonight, just to make sure you do everything right with the fawn and all?"

Wapahoo was silent a moment, seemingly deep in thought. "Okay. we can sleep out under the stars."

Wapahoo gathered up the fawn and headed for camp. Peter tugged at Sally's rope to get her to speed up her pace. Wapahoo set the fawn down, and Sally was left to wander around camp. An old woman was cleaning her pots on her knees. The goat put her head down and charged the woman, butting her in the behind, and it sent her flying. She didn't know what in the heck hit her. She was able to get to her knees when *wham!* Sally butted her again. The goat backed up for a third butt, but the elder woman was on her feet, waving a cooking pot over her head. The goat turned and ran, darting behind a redwood tree. The old woman calmly tracked down the culprit and *ka-bang* was the sound of the pot hitting poor Sally over the head. The goat let out a bellow as the old lady walked back into camp. Grandfather laughed hysterically and patted dear Sally over the head.

It was nightfall. The boys were tired and settled down to sleep. The fawn and goat lay at the end of the bearskins, plum tuckered out from the day's adventures.

Peter began to chuckle. "I bet the old goat has a headache after being hit over the head with the pot."

The boys both settled into sleep when Peter let out a big blast of bad air and then threw the bearskins over Wapahoo's head. He came out coughing and gasping for air. They laughed and told stories.

Wapahoo became serious. "Peter, there's a girl who used to live in the tribe but became missing. No one knew what happened to her. Her father and brother searched for her, but they never found her. They figured a mountain lion got her. Her mother has never been the same. She sits looking toward the field as if her daughter will come walking home."

Peter piped up, "That's sad. I wonder if it hurt real bad when the mountain lion ate her. Ooh, that sends shivers up and down my spine. The last thing you see in your whole life is the inside of a mountain lion's mouth!"

Wapahoo smiled. "She's alive, Peter. She gave me food and water in the Tolowa camp."

"Hot dang!" Peter jumped from his bed. "Why you just sittin' there? Let's go get her!"

Wapahoo knew this was impossible for just the two of them. He turned on his side and said, "I'm tired. I want to sleep."

The next morning, Wapahoo woke. It was always chilly in the morning. He pulled the bearskins up around his neck. He looked over to see if Peter was still sleeping. Peter wasn't there. Wapahoo lifted the bearskins to see if he was at the other end. Still there was no Peter.

Peter had gotten up before dawn. He saddled his horse and rode to see what he could find. He relished the chance to have a little freedom and independence. He rode on flat ground for a few hours, watching the birds fly overhead. Once in a while, a herd of deer would scatter when they saw Peter coming. Peter saw a wagon just ahead. He trotted, then galloped to meet the settlers and to say hello. There was no movement as he got closer. He saw a woman lying face down in the dirt. She had two arrows in her back and one in her leg. He rode around to the side of the old worn wagon. There was a girl who looked to be sixteen or seventeen years old. It was a gruesome sight. Her scalp was cut out, a pool of blood soaking into her clothing, straw stuffed in her head where her brains were. Peter was in Tolowa territory.

Peter swung his horse's head around and kicked her in the sides to go faster. The horse was at full speed and leaped to cross a ditch but misjudged the distance across. Both Peter and the horse fell into the ditch. The horse fell on Peter. The horse struggled to get up, waving her head and legs frantically. Peter pushed himself free. The horse jolted to her feet, limping on her right leg.

"It's okay, girl. We'll get you out of here."

Peter didn't know if the hostile Indians had seen him or not. He was nervous and feared for his life. Peter led the horse to a spot that did not have too much of an incline. The horse heaved her weight and was able to get out of the ditch by the second try.

Peter picked up the horse's right leg and examined it. "Well, it ain't broke, girl. You'll be fine." Peter patted her on the shoulder and led her away from the ditch.

Peter tried to speed the horse up but knew there was little chance of that when her leg was so badly swollen. The two traveled about an hour. Peter sat on a stump to rest. "Well, girl, we made it. We are almost home, just a while longer." Peter swatted at the flies buzzing around him. "Guess I need a bath real bad, huh, girl?'

Peter rose to his feet and looked behind him. He did not know if the Tolowa were following him or not. He pressed on with the horse limping at his side.

Chapter Six

Plas to Rescue Nay Snusie

Wapahoo was baffled as to where his new little friend could be. He figured he went back to his camp. Wapahoo heard the fawn baying for milk, as the goat was also impatient for something to eat. Wapahoo dressed. He led the goat to a bush to eat and milked her, all the while the Ned was nudging Wapahoo impatiently. He got enough milk for the baby bottle and settled Ned into his lap to feed. Ned tugged at the nipple with his mouth as to try to get it to come out faster. Wapahoo stroked his little head. He was becoming very attached.

Wapahoo heard someone coming up from behind him, and he turned to see who it was. The chief approached and sat next to him. He smiled at Wapahoo. He was proud because he had much promise as a warrior, maybe even a chief.

The chief began to speak. "Grandfather told me of your trials. I am glad the Tolowa did not take your scalp and leave you for the buzzards to feed. You have spent many days with the white boy from the wagon train. You get along well?" asked the chief.

"Yes, very well," said Wapahoo.

"Well, that is good. He does smile a lot and he has nice teeth," said the chief.

Wapahoo interrupted the chief and came right to the point. "What about Nay Snusie? Will you arrange a war party to bring her back?"

The chief became serious. "I have told Nay Snusie's mother and father that their daughter is alive and that she is held captive by the Tolowa. Tomorrow night, when the moon is full, twenty warriors will go quietly into the Tolowa camp and steal Nay Snusie back," stated the chief. "But you must stay to feed your fawn and take care of the goat with the evil spirit."

Wapahoo realized this to be good wisdom.

"There will be many war parties for you to go on, Wapahoo, in time." The chief patted him on the shoulder, took a few steps, and then, as if he remembered something else to say, he added, "Don't let the goat with the evil spirit walk with freedom in camp. The elder's nose was skinned up, and she says she will skin the goat for a rug to lay next to her bearskin blankets."

The chief walked away chuckling to himself.

Chapter Seven

Mishap at the River

Peter arrived at the river where he and Wapahoo filled the water jugs. Peter led the horse into the water to drink, holding on the reins. Peter stretched out his arms and fell listlessly into the river. The water rushed over his face, and Peter was rejuvenated. Peter, being a kind spirit and always thinking of the comfort of animals, decided to lead the horse into yet deeper water so she too could feel the cold water. The horse was unsure and put up a fight. There was a drop-off in the riverbed, and the horse's body submerged. She panicked and fought to keep her head above the water.

Peter, in all the chaos, was able to grab a hold of one of the reins and lead the horse into shallow water. "It's all right, girl, but didn't that feel refreshing! I feel like a new kid!"

The horse shook her whole body like a dog shaking the water off after a bath. She prodded the bottom of the riverbed with her hooves, her ears erect, spooking at any movement.

"I knew you would feel better. It was a little hairy, though, wasn't it, girl!"

Chapter Eight

Boar Hunt

Peter arrived at the wagon train an hour later. "What's on the spit?" he asked Rebecca.

She was the cook at Peter's camp. She hovered over the children like a chicken with chicks, making sure everyone had their tummies full. "Peter," she chided, "lunch was two hours ago. Couldn't you be here on time?"

Peter knew better than to answer as any excuse he had. He would get the dickens. Rebecca walked to the chuck wagon. Peter could hear pots and pans being tossed about. Rebecca gained her composure, stepped down from the wagon, and said thoughtfully, "You must have had a wonderful day today, so wonderful you forgot to eat." Rebecca smiled as she gathered the firewood for a fire to warm the leftover deer stew. "I don't know what we will have for supper tonight. Our food is all eaten up."

Peter slurped his lunch. He looked up from his bowl to see Rebecca glaring at him. Peter immediately sat up and ate the gentleman's way, making no more noises.

Peter thanked Rebecca and he helped her with the dishes.

Rebecca turned to Peter and asked, "Do you think you could hunt some food for us to eat tonight?"

With that last word spoken by Rebecca, Peter dropped the dish he was washing and jut off in the direction of Wapahoo's camp.

"Peter, Peter, come back here and finish the dishes!" Rebecca cried out.

"I'll do 'em later!" Peter called out.

Rebecca was exasperated. She cried out, shaking her head, "Oh, that boy. Will he ever learn his responsibilities come first? I know his dear mother has left this earth, but I ask you, Lord, will he ever learn what he has been taught?"

Peter arrived in Wapahoo's camp out of breath and excited. He saw Wapahoo sitting and holding the fawn.

"Wapahoo, you up for goin' boar hunting?" asked Peter excitedly.

Wapahoo hesitated for a moment. "Boars can kill you, Peter."

"I know, I know, you just got to outsmart them!" said Peter.

Well, Wapahoo was game. He gathered his bow and arrows. In Peter's haste, he had forgotten to bring his rifle.

"I'll be back in a minute," said Peter, and off he darted to the wagon.

Peter came running back with a pistol in his hand. "Took me a while to find the bullets," Peter said, gasping to catch his breath.

The boys head out. Peter told Wapahoo about that morning. "Now this morning, I saw some boar turds." He studied the ground. "See, there they are, right there," he said, pointing at the ground. "There're fresh, too!"

The boys looked at each other very surprised, fear showing on Wapahoo's face. They could hear snorting and squealing within earshot.

"Looks like they are hunting us! Run, run for your life!" yelled Peter.

With those last few words, Peter sprang up the tree like a mountain lion, his adrenaline pumping. He managed to jump an extra foot into the tree with ease.

Wapahoo had made it safely into another tree. The boars were sniffing the ground frantically. Wapahoo aimed his arrow at a huge boar with foot-long tusks and hit it in the shoulder. One thing about it, Wapahoo was becoming a better shot.

Peter yelled from his tree, "How many you want to get, six of them?"

They shot the sixth one and waited for the rest of the pigs to clear out, and gingerly they got down from their trees. They had to go back for help to bring the pigs back to camp, as they hadn't planned how they were going to bring them home.

After all the boars were brought back to camp, the women began the tedious task of preparing the meat. The fawn began to bay impatiently. Wapahoo stopped to milk the goat.

"Ya know, Wapahoo, the goat is probably used to the fawn by now. Maybe she will let him nurse," said Peter.

Wapahoo didn't have much faith in that idea.

"Well, it's worth a try," said Peter.

Sure enough the goat had gotten used to Ned, and she let him nurse. Peter let out a mighty "yahoo!" and danced a two-step around Wapahoo.

The elder women had the proportions of meat set out for Peter to take back to his wagon.

Chapter Nine
Peter Asks to Stay

On the way back to Wapahoo's camp, Peter became silent. Waphaoo pressed Peter to tell him what was on his mind.

Peter started out by saying, "It's a shame. I sure like living the way you do, and I ain't never had a friend as good as you. My outfit will by here until tomorrow, and then I will have to leave. I'll never see you again, Wapahoo."

Wapahoo turned to Peter and said, "Why don't you live here with me and my people?"

"Really!" Peter jumped in the air, hit the ground, and rolled into a summersault. "Yippee!" could be heard for a good mile.

"Where are your mother and father, Peter?' asked Wapahoo.

"Oh." Peter put his head down, looking at the ground. He looked up at Wapahoo with tears in his eyes. "My mother died from the fever, and my father died not long after I was born."

"How come you are with the wagon train?" asked Wapahoo.

"My mother is a Baptist and when the minister offered to take the saints to more religious surroundings, my mother and the others decided it was the best thing for our future." Peter continued speaking. "There were a lot of outlaws where we were from, so Mother felt we were no longer safe." He wiped the tears from his eyes and said, "But hey, look, I wouldn't trade meeting you for all the candy in the mercantile and even if all the chocolate was from Switzerland!"

The boys set out to find Chief Ha-go-I-neigh and to ask his permission to let Peter live in the tribe. The chief opened Peter's mouth and looked inside to see Peter's teeth, then he felt up and down his arm. The chief was silent.

Peter began to squirm. He whispered to Wapahoo, "What if he says I am too small?"

Wapahoo hushed Peter as they both waited for the answer.

"Wapahoo, you will need to feed him more food to make him a strong brave," said the chief.

Wapahoo smiled at Peter and Peter extended his hand to the chief to shake, but the chief just smiled.

"Thank you, thank you so much!" cried Peter.

For the boys, their next mission was to get permission from the Baptist minister. They found Sam Tyler passed out in his wagon with a bottle of whiskey by his side.

Peter was very disappointed. "We well have to wait until he comes to. Come on, Wapahoo. Let's get my belongings from the other wagon."

He packed his clothes and specifically looked for the locket that was left to himby his deceased mother. He clutched the locket for a few moments, deep in thought. He opened it. "This is my mother," Peter told Wapahoo. Peter packed three of the books he and his mother had been reading since they joined the wagon train. "Maybe I can teach you how to read, Wapahoo. You can travel to all kinds of places. It feels like you are right there in those places just by reading words," stated Peter.

Wapahoo didn't say anything, but he looked a little curious.

"Let's go and check on Sam Tyler," said Peter.

The preacher was sitting up, holding his head in agony.

"Mr. Tyler, seeing as I have no living kin on this here wagon expedition and being an orphan, I have made the decision to live with Wapahoo and the Yurok people."

The preacher began to burp uncontrollably. He jumped to his feet, pushed the boys out of his way, and leaned over the wagon, heaving over and over again. Pale, he turned and looked at the boys, wiping his mouth. He said, "You will probably be safer with the Yurok than you would be with us. Good luck, my boy, and hang on to your top knot!" said Sam as he staggered back to his bed. "I wished I felt better." Burping again, Sam yelled out, "Don't forget to pack your belongings, Peter!"

"Already done, sir!" Peter called out as he jumped off the wagon, narrowly missing the spit-up. "Ooh, yuck, watch your step, Wapahoo!"

Chapter Ten

Wapahoo and Peter's Lone
Try to Rescue Nay Snusie

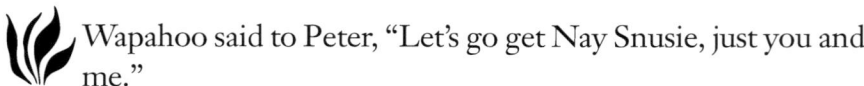Wapahoo said to Peter, "Let's go get Nay Snusie, just you and me."

Peter didn't hesitate a minute. He replied, "Absolutely. Let's go tonight after everyone is asleep."

The boys packed the supplies they would need and waited until everyone went to bed. Wapahoo told Peter to bring the horses to the clearing and wait for him there. Peter obeyed. He was anxious and excited to meet Nay Snusie. They set out using the moonlight to show them the way to the Tolowa camp.

"Peter," Wapahoo said, "how do we get Nay Snusie to come with us?"

"I don't know, you're the Indian, Wapahoo. You're supposed to know how to sneak up on someone and hold them captive. I am just a farmer's boy," said Peter.

Wapahoo thought for a moment. "I think I know which plank house she is in, Peter. Oh, I don't think this is a good idea after all. Let's go back before we get hurt," said Wapahoo.

"Come on, Wapahoo. This is adventurous! How can I write a really good book if nothing exciting happens in it? The only ones who will read it will be you and me, and that's only if you learn to read. I have the perfect title, too, *The Wondrous Journeys of Wapahoo and Peter.* Pretty catchy, don't ya think?" said Peter with a grin.

Wapahoo didn't reply; he was too worried about the situation they got themselves into.

Against Wapahoo's better judgment, the pair proceeded to the Tolowa camp.

"Well, we better make a plan, then," said Wapahoo.

"Shh! Did you hear that?" asked Peter.

"No," said Wapahoo. "Hear what?"

Peter halted his horse, and the two stood their horses still and listened. A bear barreled out from behind the redwood trees. Wapahoo reached for his spear and Peter for his pistol. Wapahoo's horse reared and sent him to the ground, and he lost grip of his spear. The bear snorted and pounded the dirt with his massive paw. He rose to stand on his back legs and swiped Wapahoo across the chest with a mighty blow. Peter aimed his pistol and pulled the trigger. His horse reared, knocking Peter on top of the bear. The bear fell limp not far from Wapahoo.

Chapter Eleven
Tolowa Capture Wapahoo and Peter

Someone else was within earshot of the fight between the bear and the boys. Six Tolowa warriors watched as Wapahoo and Peter took on the bear. The boys were big medicine because of their age, strength, and courage. To a point, the braves were afraid. They figured the boys might have been given power from the great spirit to be able to conquer their bear brother. One warrior began circling the two boys. Wapahoo knew their fate would be death. He felt lightheaded from loss of blood and collapsed onto the ground, leaving poor Peter to witness their capture.

Two warriors retrieved the boys' horses and slapped Wapahoo's belly down across the horses' backs. They tied Peter's hands with rope and pulled him from behind the horse. Peter was very wise as not to lose his footing, as he feared he would be dragged to death.

The warriors tied the boys to two trees in the Tolowa camp, and there they stayed the rest of the night.

The sun rose and the children ran to see who was captured. They began throwing rocks and hitting Peter and Wapahoo with the sticks they picked up.

Peter looked over at his dear friend. "How are you doing? Do you hurt pretty bad? What do you think they will do to us?"

Wapahoo, being wise and older, did not want to scare his little friend. He did not want Peter to know what the Tolowa did to their enemies. "I don't know, Peter," was all Wapahoo said.

The boys watched as the people went throughout their daily chores. Nay Snusie stepped out from her shank house, shooing a child away from the entrance.

"Look, Peter! There is Nay Snusie!" exclaimed Wapahoo.

Peter strained to see her. "Well, she ain't much to look at, is she? I think the one by the fire pit is much cuter. Why don't we take her with us, too, if we ever live long enough to get out of here," sighed Peter. But the soberness of the situation brought Peter back into reality. "Oh, how I wish I had listened to you, Wapahoo. We should have turned around and went back home when you wanted to."

Nay Snusie gathered a water jug and headed to the river to fill it up. She returned offering Wapahoo a drink of cool water and ignored Peter.

Peter became indignant. "She didn't give me any water, and I am so thirsty." He figured he would use his charm with the gal he thought was cute by the fire pit.

Peter smiled a big toothy grin at her and asked Wapahoo, "How do you say 'You're cute, and could you bring me some water?'" He nodded his head at her and motioned her to come over with his eyes.

The maiden looked to see if anyone was watching and then she slowly walked to Peter.

Wapahoo spoke slowly, telling Peter the correct words. Peter repeated the words twice to himself before he attempted to say the words to the girl. He smiled at her and she smiled shyly, blushing a bit, and then she walked to the river for water and returned, giving Peter a drink.

The girls returned shortly, giggling as they approached. They offered the boys food this time. After the girls had fed the boys, they walked away, talking and giggling, looking over their shoulders at the two boys.

"Wapahoo, I got bad news. I got to pee."

Wapahoo rolled his eyes.

"Seriously, Wapo, what do I do? Hey, that's what I will call you from now on, 'Wapo.' Your name is just too long for my liking," said Peter. "Anyway," Peter said impatiently, "what do I do?"

"Just pee," said Wapahoo.

It was a gusher. A huge amount of urine ran down Peter's leg, splatting on the ground.

"What a relief," stated Peter.

A few moments later, a huge puddle gathered at Wapahoo's feet. The boys chuckled but quickly resumed their composure and fear when two strapping warriors walked toward them, eyes black as their souls. Both warriors were clutching hunting knives. Fear rippled through their bodies, as he knew this moment would come.

The larger of the two warriors grabbed a fistful of hair and slowly began to scalp Peter. Peter screamed in agony. Wapahoo looked on with empathy in his heart, wanting so badly to protect his little friend from the excruciating pain, but he knew he could do nothing for Peter.

A crowd gathered to watch the barbaric torture. Blood saturated Peter's clothing, and he lost all consciousness. The next warrior stood in front of Wapahoo, and he studied his wounds for a moment. The warrior raised his knife to Wapahoo's chest and began to slice into the open lesions he received from the bear attack the previous night. Wapahoo chanted his death song, but there came hope into the boys' frightening situation.

An arrow flew through the air and hit one of the warriors in the skull, killing him instantly.

From behind trees, bushes, rocks, and shrubs, the mighty Yurok bravely ascended into battle, faces painted for war, armed with courage and outrage of the many years of hatred they had harbored for the Tolowa. Chief Ha-go-I-neigh cut the boys' ropes, and two warriors took the boys safely to the river.

Wapahoo was able to tell the chief which one was Nay Snusie and then described the girl Peter liked and said to bring her, too.

There is much bloodshed, but mostly to the Tolowa, as they were not prepared for the attack. It was not hard for the chief to find Nay Snusie, as she had not changed that much in the three years she went missing. Nay Snusie seemed almost relieved to be captured by her former tribe. She did not put up a fight.

The chief was a little confused as to who the girl Peter wanted was. He thought he might have the right girl, so he caught her and threw her over his shoulder, the girl kicking and biting like a wild animal. An arrow soared down and pierced the girl in the rump. She screamed and began to cry.

The Yurok made a hasty retreat to the river. Peter was still unconscious and draped across a horse's back, with one of the warriors steering the horse. The chief dragged the girl to Wapahoo.

Wapahoo asked, "Who is this?'

"This is the girl you asked for, isn't it?" said the chief.

"You got the wrong girl," said Wapahoo.

So the chief shrugged his shoulders and turned loose the girl. She ran away crying, stumbling over the river rocks. The warriors helped Nay Snusie onto the chief's horse and the little band galloped toward Yurok territory.

Chapter Twelve

Escape from the Tolowa

Wapahoo was among the warriors in the lead. He head off on the path alone and galloped to the proximity of the dead bear Peter killed. Wapahoo's judgment as to where the bear was wasn't far off the mark. A badger was feeding on the bear, and he put up a ferocious fight defending what he felt was his. Wapahoo didn't want to have to kill the badger; he knew he was just trying to survive. He threw rocks, sticks, and branches, but that didn't seem to run the badger off.

Regretfully Wapahoo armed himself with his spear. At first he poked the animal. It just made the badger all the more fierce in his attempt to keep his kill. Wapahoo began to talk to the badger. He whispered a prayer to the great spirit that the animal would leave, so Wapahoo waited a little while longer, and luckily the badger was full and he wandered off, growling with his every step.

Wapahoo quickly cut the paw off of the bear, placed it in his sack, got up on his horse, and galloped off toward Yurok land. He stopped at a ridge to scope out where his people were. It was as if a dust storm was below, but actually it was the Tolowa in pursuit of the Yurok. Wapahoo galloped west and took the long way back to his camp.

The two divisions entered onto Yurok land, and the warriors could see their camp not far off. The remaining Yurok in camp saw the situation and quickly mounted their horses, ready for battle, waving their spears in the air and yelling the war cry. The warriors sped past the chief and others toward the Tolowas. The Tolowa were outnumbered. They made a retreat back to their land. The Yurok chased them as far as Tolowa territory, and then they returned home. This time they beat the Tolowa, but next time, they might not be so lucky.

Chapter Thirteen
Peter May Not Survive

Shi-kies and the medicine man tended to Peter and his injury.

Peter said to Shi-kies, "Did we whip them?"

"Yes, Peter, they are whipped."

Peter was placed on the bearskins. The elders tended to his wounds for three days. Peter sunk in and out of consciousness, delirious from the fever he had contracted. Infection had spread, and the medicine man sprinkled tobacco and other concoctions of herbs and roots over Peter's body. They waited.

Wapahoo had much faith in the great spirit. He stayed in the sweat house, cleansing his spirit, asking the great spirit to save Peter's life. There was much worry in the tribe. The people had come to love and respect the boy named Peter. They did not want to see the young boy die.

On the fourth day, Peter's fever broke. Nay Snusie called for Wapahoo. Peter was sitting up and smiling weakly as Wapahoo entered the room.

Wapahoo proudly dropped the bear claw on the ground.

"How on earth did you get the bear claw, Wapoo?" asked Peter inquisitively.

"I will tell you of the events when you are back to yourself, Peter," said Wapahoo.

"Fine, keep me in suspense. I'll just have to get better quick so I can hear how we whipped them lazy bastards."

"How's your head feel, Peter?" asked Wapahoo.

"It sure hurts. Is there a lot of hair missing?" whined Peter.

"Some. You'll have a nice scar to show all the girls," said Wapahoo.

"Yeah, that always gets 'em," sighed Peter. "I think I'll rest now, Wapo. I am tired. Oh, did the wagon train move on?" he asked.

"Yes, they said to bid you farewell," said Wapahoo.

"Goodnight, Wapo. Thanks for being my friend. Oh, just one more thing. Did we get Nay Snusie?" asked Peter.

"Yes, Peter, we got Nay Snusie," said Wapahoo.

"Good, 'cause I'd hate to lose my top knot for nothing. Now I got a semi-bald head to show for it!" chuckled Peter. "Were her parents glad to see her?" asked Peter.

Peter is definitely lightheaded from the loss of blood and fever and a little crazy now, thought Wapahoo. "Yes, her parents were glad to see her. Now you rest. I need to take care of Ned and Sally," stated Wapahoo, thinking he could go on to the chores at hand.

Peter asked yet another question. "One last thing, Wapo." Wapahoo sort of snapped. "What?"

"I love you," said Peter sheepishly. "Geez, I've gone nuts."

Chapter Fifteen
Beaver Dam

Summer was coming to an end, and Peter had healed nicely, sporting a six-inch scar on top of his head. The boys invited the children to play in the field with the deerskin ball Grandfather had made for them to play with. The group played ball, but every time the children bent over to pick up the ball, Sally butted them, and pretty soon it was more fun to get butted than it was to play with the ball. The children, Ned and Sally, tired of the game.

"Hey, everybody, let's go swimming!" yelled out Peter.

And off they went, stirring up dust like a herd of buffalo charging across the prairie. They arrived at the river, and a turtle quickly rushed into the water. One of the children ran to catch it, falling in headfirst and then surfacing, laughing at his situation.

Peter floated downstream by himself, and he came to a beaver den. Peter had always wondered what the inside of a beaver den looked like, so down he went to explore. He popped his head up in the den to see a mother beaver's black eyes glaring at him. She began growling, and there by her side were two kits. Peter didn't hesitate a second. He reached out to snatch one to take home to raise. Mother beaver lunged at Peter's hand and bit down on his little finger, taking it clean off. Peter screamed in pain and he punched the inside of the dam, causing some damage. He swam to one side, then to the other. The water was murky and bloody. He couldn't see his way out of the den. Mother beaver was moving closer to enter into the water. Peter grabbed a branch and hit her, trying in desperation to keep her from biting him again.

Peter panicked. He latched onto a stick and began beating a hole in the cavity of the den. The den was so intricately woven that it was difficult to penetrate. He hit mother beaver again and again until she retreated some, leaving Peter to work his way through the branches and wood. It was no good. The wood was too thick to penetrate without a hatchet.

For fear he would not survive, he submerged himself into the water again and frantically he pulled the wood with all his might and was free. Mother beaver entered the water again after Peter. Peter swam with all the strength he had back to the shore, mother beaver following behind him.

Peter ran past the others and called out, "We got to go!" Everyone saw the blood and asked no questions. They got out of the water in a frenzy, and everyone ran home, Ned and Sally trailing behind.